Rhyme
Time

Lighthouse
Mouse

First published in 2006 by
Franklin Watts
338 Euston Road
London
NW1 3BH

Franklin Watts Australia
Hachette Children's Books
Level 17/207 Kent Street
Sydney
NSW 2000

A CIP catalogue record for this book is available
from the British Library.

ISBN 978 0 7496 6815 0

Series Editor: Jackie Hamley
Series Advisor: Dr Barrie Wade
Series Designer: Peter Scoulding

Printed in China

Franklin Watts is a division of
Hachette Children's Books,
an Hachette UK company
www.hachette.co.uk

Lighthouse
Mouse

by Anne Adeney

Illustrated by Lisa Smith

W
FRANKLIN WATTS
LONDON•SYDNEY

Here is the lighthouse,
red and white,

warning ships with its
flashing light.

Jake climbs steps that get steeper and steeper.

That's his job – he's the
lighthouse keeper.

He lives here with just his ferns,

stacks of books

and flocks of terns.

Jake doesn't know
he's not alone.

Someone else calls the
lighthouse "home".

11

From his little
hole he peers,
bright, black eyes
and great big ears.

12

When Jake's food comes
by rowing boat,

Ben's Boat

there's a surprise
beneath Ben's coat.

The lighthouse mouse
quivers with fear.

16

"A cat will surely
find me here!"

Cat's eyes light up
as she smells Mouse.

She runs all over
the lighthouse.

Under the bed,

behind the clock,

20

through the kitchen

and round the rock.

Mouse crept to his
hole as Cat napped.

Cat woke and pounced!

Mouse was trapped!

But Cat did not bite,
scratch or hiss.

Instead, she gave
Mouse a little kiss.

"Jake's busy.

His work never ends."

"It's lonely here,
can we be friends?"

Leapfrog Rhyme Time has been specially designed to fit the requirements of the Literacy Framework. It offers real books for beginner readers by top authors and illustrators.

RHYME TIME

Mr Spotty's Potty
ISBN 978 0 7496 3831 3

Eight Enormous Elephants
ISBN 978 0 7496 4634 9

Freddie's Fears
ISBN 978 0 7496 4382 9

Squeaky Clean
ISBN 978 0 7496 6805 1

Craig's Crocodile
ISBN 978 0 7496 6806 8

Felicity Floss: Tooth Fairy
ISBN 978 0 7496 6807 5

Captain Cool
ISBN 978 0 7496 6808 2

Monster Cake
ISBN 978 0 7496 6809 9

The Super Trolley Ride
ISBN 978 0 7496 6810 5

The Royal Jumble Sale
ISBN 978 0 7496 6811 2

But, Mum!
ISBN 978 0 7496 6812 9

Dan's Gran's Goat
ISBN 978 0 7496 6814 3

Lighthouse Mouse
ISBN 978 0 7496 6815 0

Big Bad Bart
ISBN 978 0 7496 6816 7

Ron's Race
ISBN 978 0 7496 6817 4

Woolly the Bully
ISBN 978 0 7496 7098 6*
ISBN 978 0 7496 7790 9

Boris the Spider
ISBN 978 0 7496 7099 3*
ISBN 978 0 7496 7791 6

Miss Polly's Seaside Brolly
ISBN 978 0 7496 7100 6*
ISBN 978 0 7496 7792 3

Juggling Joe
ISBN 978 0 7496 7103 7*
ISBN 978 0 7496 7795 4

What a Frog!
ISBN 978 0 7496 7102 0*
ISBN 978 0 7496 7794 7

The Lonely Pirate
ISBN 978 0 7496 7101 3*
ISBN 978 0 7496 7793 0

I Wish!
ISBN 978 0 7496 7940 8*
ISBN 978 0 7496 7952 1

Raindrop Bill
ISBN 978 0 7496 7941 5*
ISBN 978 0 7496 7953 8

Sir Otto
ISBN 978 0 7496 7942 2*
ISBN 978 0 7496 7954 5

Queen Rosie
ISBN 978 0 7496 7943 9*
ISBN 978 0 7496 7955 2

Giraffe's Good Game
ISBN 978 0 7496 7944 6*
ISBN 978 0 7496 7956 9

Miss Lupin's Motorbike
ISBN 978 0 7496 7945 3*
ISBN 978 0 7496 7957 6

Alfie the Sea Dog
ISBN 978 0 7496 7946 0*
ISBN 978 0 7496 7958 3

Red Riding Hood Rap
ISBN 978 0 7496 7947 7*
ISBN 978 0 7496 7959 0

Pets on Parade
ISBN 978 0 7496 7948 4*
ISBN 978 0 7496 7960 6

Let's Dance
ISBN 978 0 7496 7949 1*
ISBN 978 0 7496 7961 3

Benny and the Monster
ISBN 978 0 7496 7950 7*
ISBN 978 0 7496 7962 0

Bathtime Rap
ISBN 978 0 7496 7951 4*
ISBN 978 0 7496 7963 7

Other Leapfrog titles also available:

Leapfrog Fairy Tales

A selection of favourite fairy tales, simply retold.

Leapfrog

Fun, original stories by top authors and illustrators.

For more details go to:

www.franklinwatts.co.uk